P9-ELW-713

Amelia's

DATE DUE

SEP 10 2008	FEB 0 7 2012
OCT 1 6 2008	MAR 1 6 2012
DEC 19 2008	MAY 0 9 2012
MAR 1 4 2009	
APR 1 1 2009	
JUL 1 5 2009	
AUG 2 1 2009	
SEP 0 3 2009	
JUN 2 3 2010	
JUL 0 8 2010	
AUG 1 6 2010	
AUG 3 0 2011	
AUG 3 0 2011	
OCT 2 6 2011	
JAN 0 9 2012	

(ex   'UCH!-

Simon &   ers

I'd l

New York   London   Toronto   Sydney

...and here ... and here!

Plainville Public Library
56 East Main Street
Plainville, Conn. 06062

This guide is dedicated to Lisa,
because big kids can be just as tricky
to watch as little ones.

↑ and you have to move faster!

SIMON & SCHUSTER BOOKS FOR YOUNG READERS
An imprint of Simon & Schuster Children's Publishing Division
1230 Avenue of the Americas, New York, New York 10020
Copyright © 2008 by Marissa Moss

All rights reserved, including the right of reproduction in whole
or in part in any form.

SIMON & SCHUSTER BOOKS FOR YOUNG READERS
IS A TRADEMARK of SIMON & SCHUSTER, INC.

Amelia® and the notebook design are
registered trademarks of Marissa Moss.

A Paula Wiseman Book
Book design by Amelia
(with help from Lucy Ruth Cummins)
The text for this book is hand-lettered.
Manufactured in China
2 4 6 8 10 9 7 5 3 1

CIP data for this book is available from the
Library of Congress.

ISBN-13: 978-1-4169-5051-6
ISBN-10: 1-4169-5051-6

She even
changed
a soggy
diaper!

first
edition

6/08   3 2535 11252 9067

Amelia's Guide to Babysitting

WAAAAH!

I know there's an answer in here somewhere.

I just better find it QUICK!

I've tried a lot of ways to make money. Dog walking was a disaster! The dogs ended up walking me instead of the other way around.

Selling lemonade went sour. The only people who ended up drinking it were me and Carly, my best friend and business partner.

So when Carly said she had a great idea for how we could make LOTS of money AND have fun together at the same time, I was all ears.

Now that we're older, we can do jobs we couldn't do before.

Like babysitting! My brothers earn big bucks that way.

Babysitting! Of course! My sister, Cleo, babysits a lot and she <u>always</u> has money, like Carly's brothers do. And I even have some experience (unlike the dog-walking fiasco, where I had <u>no</u> idea what I was getting myself into since I've never owned a dog). I've taken care of my baby half brother a few times. I didn't get paid, but it still counts as experience.

George is my half brother (not half <u>of</u> a brother) because my dad remarried and started a new family. They don't live close by — in fact, they're an airplane ride away in Chicago — but whenever I visit, I end up watching George, which is okay because he's very cute and I love him.

Having experience means I know how much work babysitting is — it's not exactly a walk in the park. I don't mind (too much) with George because he's my half brother (and he's so much nicer than my whole sister). But it's still not easy. When he was really little, I had a hard time guessing what he wanted when he cried. It's better now that he can talk, but it's still exhausting. So I wasn't sure about Carly's idea.

"I dunno," I told her. "Babysitting is work!"

"Jobs usually are. If it wasn't, why would someone pay you?"

She had a point. I admit when I first imagined taking care of George, I thought he would just smile or sleep the whole time. He didn't do either.

Wouldn't it be great to get paid to do nothing — just to be there in case of emergency, which, of course, would never actually happen? After all, it's called babysitting, so it should involve resting and relaxing, not ← running around.

Baby's asleep somewhere over here. ↘

"Anyway," said Carly, "it's not <u>hard</u> work. Especially if we do it together — then it'll be FUN!"

"But what if I don't like the kid?" I asked. "George can drive me crazy, but he's my brother, so I <u>have</u> to put up with him."

"Don't worry about liking the kid. You can stand <u>anyone</u> for a short time. After all, you <u>live</u> with Cleo and you survived the mean Mr. L. for a teacher last year."

She was right, but those people were <u>bad</u> examples. I didn't have a choice about Cleo or Mr. L. — believe me, if I had, things would be way better! With the kids we babysat, I could always say no. I might <u>want</u> to say no.

"Okay," Carly tried again. "Think of it this way — do you like <u>money</u>?"

I felt sorry for my empty piggy bank. He deserved a meal or two. That was worth dealing with a baby Cleo or Mr. L.

Remember, you said you'd feed me!

"And we'll be working together," Carly added. "That makes anything easier to face."

That convinced me. I can handle tough stuff if I have Carly's help. One thing that made Mr. L.'s meanness so extra mean was that Carly wasn't in that class with me.

"You're right," I said. "Count me in!"

So it's set. We're starting a babysitting business where we always work together. That means only earning half as much money, since we'll split it, but it'll be <u>twice</u> as much fun. Thats the kind of math I like!

DOU BB LE BEE'S

2 BABYSITTERS FOR THE PRICE OF 1!

Day or night! Call 831-0602   Night or day!

Carly wants to call us the Double Bee's. She's even designed a flyer to put up on the library bulletin board to drum up business. She was all prepared before she asked me!

I know Carly can handle anything. That's just the kind of person she is. But I'm not so sure if I'll be a great babysitter. Before we start, I want to be prepared too, so I'm making this guide. By the time I'm done, I'll know how to handle finicky eaters and bath times, tantrums and hiccups — everything a babysitter might need!

Carly says she'll help.

We're partners, so let's make this guide together. I'm good at research — I'll ask people what tips they have for better babysitting.

And I'll make charts, quizzes, and lists. We'll be super-prepared, ready for ANYTHING.

When Cleo saw what we were working on, she laughed. She said those who can, do. Those who can't, make guides and tell other people what to do. She said we don't need a guide, we need experience. Kids are going to run us ragged. That's what she thinks! I told her we'd show her how wrong she is.

Tell you what — you want to prove me wrong, I'll give you a chance to. I'm supposed to babysit for the Reeses this Saturday. I'll tell them I can't but you can.

Our first job already?! Carly and I didn't think twice. We both said, "Great, we'll do it!" But then I wondered, what if Cleo is setting us up? What if the Reese kids are horrible brats?

It was as if Cleo could read my mind.
↓

And don't worry — the Reese kids aren't monsters. They're just normal kids. Ruthy is 5 and Tyler is 7. How hard can it be?

It sounded good, except how come _now_ she was saying how easy it would be when before she said it would be too hard for us? I guess we'd just have to find out. If it was a set-up, at least Carly would be there to help me out — and we'd _never_ trust Cleo again.

So it's all set. In three days we have our first real job!

I wanted to find out <u>before</u> our job what kind of babysitter I would be, so I made a quiz to see if I'm like Cleo, Gigi, Carly, or Leah. If it turns out I'm like Cleo, I should quit now, but if I'm like Carly, I'm ready for anything.

QUIZ #1

WHAT KIND OF BABYSITTER ARE YOU?
(for older kids, not babies)

② As a special treat, you're willing to:

ⓐ let them eat cookies so long as they do it OUTSIDE.	ⓑ do a fun art project.	ⓒ play a game so long as you can watch TV at the same time.	ⓓ let them help with your homework.

③ How do you handle dinner?

ⓐ Quickly and efficiently.	ⓑ Warm and friendly.	ⓒ Casually and easily.	ⓓ Sloppily, but it's not your kitchen, so who cares?

④ What best describes your attitude toward bath time?

| ⓐ Scrub, scrub, scrub! | ⓑ Add lots of bubble bath to make extra fun. | ⓒ A washcloth wipe is good enough. | ⓓ The kids aren't _that_ dirty - why bother? |

⑤ Name one of your favorite things to do while babysitting.

| ⓐ Organizing closets. | ⓑ Playing with all the toys you remember from when you were little. | ⓒ Your nails. | ⓓ Watching TV even if it's kiddie cartoons. |

⑥ What is the best way to deal with a temper tantrum?

ⓐ Tidy up the place.	ⓑ Calmly but firmly.	ⓒ Lock yourself in the bathroom.	ⓓ Panic and call 911.

⑦ What is the best way to handle discipline?

ⓐ Avoid kids who need it.	ⓑ Calmly but firmly.	ⓒ With an iron fist.	ⓓ By yelling.

⑧ What do you like to read to the kid before bed time?

ⓐ A book that hasn't been drooled or chewed on.	ⓑ As many books as possible – it's fun to do the different voices.	ⓒ The shortest book in the house.	ⓓ Your own book, to yourself.

⑨ How do you put a child to bed?

ⓐ With the least fuss possible.	ⓑ With a story or a lullaby.	ⓒ Pull back covers, insert child, pull up covers.	ⓓ As soon as possible. Right after dinner is the best.

If you answered mostly a's, you have a lot of potential as a babysitter, but you need to relax and not worry about messes so much. With little kids, they're hard to avoid. You're a neat freak, like Leah (the kind of person who folds underwear).

If you answered mostly b's, you're a terrific babysitter for any age! You have a lot of patience and genuinely like little kids. You're like Carly.

I didn't answer all b's, but enough so that I'm here — that's good news!

If you answered mostly c's, you need to think less about yourself and more about the kid you're taking care of. You could be great at this job if you'd just try to have more fun (the kind a little kid can enjoy). Still, you do the job fine. You're like Gigi.

If you answered mostly d's, you're doing the bare minimum. Why don't you find work that fits better with your personality, something where you won't hurt kids' feelings, something more impersonal, like filing papers or hoeing weeds? You're not nice enough to be a good babysitter. You're like Cleo.

What do you know? Kids LOVE me!

I did so well on the quiz, I felt pretty confident about our job. I could tell Carly wasn't worried at all.

Saturday at 1 p.m. we walked over to the Reeses (they live 3 doors down — very convenient). The mom and dad seemed very nice, the house was clean and organized, and the kids seemed really sweet. Plus the parents left us brownies and pizza to eat — I grade them an A+ for that.

Ruthy just wanted us to read books to her.

Tyler wanted help building with Legos.

They were both completely easy to take care of. All we had to do was play with them. They even put away their toys when we asked them to. I didn't have to worry about not liking them or that they wouldn't like me. It was all a piece of cake.

In fact, it was so easy, I thought there was no point to finishing the guide. I mean, there's nothing to babysitting. I was worried for nothing. I couldn't wait to tell Cleo how wrong she was.

And she couldn't wait to hear how it went. As soon as we got home, Cleo was there, asking us questions.

"So," she said. "Not as easy as you thought, eh?"

Carly laughed. "You're right — it wasn't. It was even _easier_! Those kids are great and the parents are the kind you _want_ to babysit for."

Cleo looked surprised. Then she smiled. "Well, if it was like that, you won't mind babysitting them again _next_ Saturday, only this time, it's all day, from 7 a.m. to around midnight. Think you're up for that?"

Carly and I looked at each other. We didn't see trouble — we saw dollar signs! This was WAY better than trying to sell lemonade.

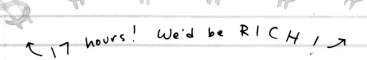

↲ 17 hours! We'd be R I C H ! ↗

"You really don't mind giving us your job?" Carly asked. "That's a lot of money."

"I know," said Cleo, "but I really want to go to a concert with Gigi. You'd be doing me a favor."

Since she put it that way, naturally we said yes. Now our problem is deciding what to do with all the money we'll make. I _love_ having that kind of problem.

Now I think I'll keep making the guide anyway. Not because babysitting is hard, but because there are lots of things you need to know about when you babysit, including stuff that has nothing to do with the kids. Like food. What kind of snacks are available is more important than it might seem.

RATE THE SNACKAGE QUOTIENT

HIGH — The best, meaning the tastiest snacks around. Chips, microwave popcorn, pretzels — salty foods are GOOD! Ice cream is also good so long as it's a flavor like Chocolate Fudge, not a strange grown-up flavor like Maple.

↑
The highest rating — the Full Tummy.

MEDIUM — Okay, there are lots of healthy foods like fruit and carrots, but there's also cheese and crackers and chocolate-chip cookies. If there's chocolate, there's hope.

↑
The next-best rating — the No-Complaints Tummy.

LOW – The worst possible choices, meaning
food that has all the flavor sucked out
of it, like all-organic, vegan snacks.
No bread, cheese, chips, nothing with
any taste to it. Quinoa pretzels are
probably the best you'll get here, but
what _is_ quinoa and is it really edible?

The worst
rating – the
Hollow Tummy

Homes with a high snackage quotient are an
automatic yes if they ask you to babysit.

Homes with a medium snackage quotient are
a possible yes, depending on other factors, like how
bratty the kids are, whether they have cable TV,
how desperately you want the money, that kind of
thing.

Homes with a low snackage quotient are a probable
no, but if there's something else really great about the
family, you could still say yes. If they have a great DVD
collection, if they have a hot tub you can use once the
kids are asleep — those are good reasons to overlook the
poor snackage.

you can always
bring your own. →

Emergency Snackage Kit

Nacho fixin's all
included along with
↙ some microwave
popcorn and 3
kinds of
cookies.

That made me wonder.
↓

QUIZ #2

WHAT MATTERS MOST WHEN YOU'RE BABYSITTING?

① Good snacks? Which of these is a deal breaker, meaning no babysitting, no way?

② The amount you're paid? How little are you willing to accept?

③ Easy kids? Where do you draw the line on difficult behavior?

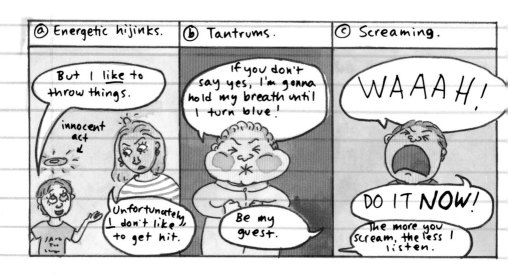

④ Home entertainment? Do you need a big-screen TV or does a radio satisfy you? What's the least you'll accept?

If you answered mostly a's, you need a comfortable situation for babysitting to be worth your while. You'd rather be at home or out with friends than face the smallest difficulties.

you shouldn't take any job dealing with customer service. Handling cranky people is NOT for you.

If you answered mostly b's, you're focused on your goals and don't let annoyance get in the way of earning good money. You can babysit under less-than-ideal circumstances.

I put myself here.
Some things aren't worth any amount of money, but I'm not lazy.

If you answered mostly c's, you like a challenge. You might want to join the Peace Corps when you're older or take the kind of job that offers hazard pay – you're willing to face the nitty-gritty. You could even babysit the Terrible Toroni Triplets.

Or you could be a substitute teacher. You have a strong stomach for rude kids.

MINE!

NO, MINE!

NO, MINE!

Definitely NOT mine!

This is where Carly is. Nothing scares her. So what happens if I'm not up to her level? What if I can't take the Terrible Toroni Triplets?

I gave Carly the test to see what mattered most to her. She said money, just as I expected. She can handle ANYTHING so long as she's paid enough.

I can deal with a brat, no problem. But it's got to be worth my while. The Reeses are an example of a perfect job because they pay well, they have a nice, comfortable home with good snacks, and the kids are easy.

I agree with Carly, except I'm sure there are some kids I wouldn't want to babysit no matter how much I was paid. What if I had to take care of Baby Cleo? Or imagine the mean Mr. L. as a toddler. Forget it!

Goo!

I bet she bit and scratched and screamed and stank and EVERYTHING you don't want in a baby! Plus she was Cleo — enough said!

Which made me think, how bratty does a kid have to be to make the money not worth it? And if a kid is really horrible, is there <u>some</u> amount of money that would make it bearable? I mean, everything has its price. Do <u>I</u> have a price?

It seems like everyone has a different range for tolerating brats. Carly's is high, but mine is pretty low. Does that make us a good or bad team? Carly thinks it doesn't matter because her being with me will make it easier for me to put up with nasty kids. I'm not so sure.

What if I disappoint Carly by making _her_ deal with the brat?

What if she thinks I don't deserve half the money? Will that start a fight?

Suddenly babysitting reminded me of why I hate team sports - I'm always afraid I'll let the team down and they'll lose, all because of me.

What if being around me makes the bad kid act even worse? Will Carly blame me?

Can we be friends _and_ business partners or will working together ruin our friendship?

I didn't tell Carly my worries because she says it's exhausting to reassure me when I'm like that, and it's a waste of time to worry about something that hasn't happened yet. But that's what worrying is — fretting over the future. Once it becomes the present, you don't worry — you react (sad, mad, relieved). Whatever it is, at least you're no longer worried. It's the unknown element, not being sure exactly what to expect, that makes me nervous. I feel like it's all a big gamble whether you deal with brats or not.

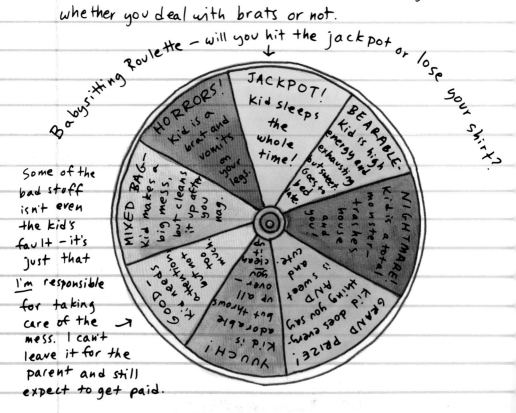

Babysitting Roulette — will you hit the jackpot or lose your shirt?

↓

JACKPOT! Kid sleeps the whole time!

HORRORS! Kid is a brat and vomits on your legs.

BEARABLE. Kid is high energy and exhausting but sweet. Gets to bed late.

NIGHTMARE! Kid is a total monster — trashes house AND is sweet AND cute and over it! clean — up!

MIXED BAG! Kid makes a big mess, but cleans it up after you nag.

GOOD! Kid needs attention but not too much.

YUUCH! Kid is adorable but throws up all over — you clean it up!

GRAND PRIZE! Kid does everything you say AND

Some of the bad stuff isn't even the kid's fault — it's just that I'm <u>responsible</u> for taking care of the mess. I can't leave it for the parent and still expect to get paid.

At dinner, Cleo kept on asking questions about the Reeses, like she couldn't believe Carly and me had it so easy. Was she trying to scare me about Saturday's job or was she just jealous? I definitely wasn't going to tell her about my worries. No matter what, I wanted Cleo to think I was totally in control and that babysitting was a snap for me. Even if I wasn't and it wasn't.

And Mrs. Reese didn't ask you to do any ironing? Or to clean the oven? She didn't treat you like a maid?

Nope, nope, nope. All we did was play with the kids. It was easy pay — like taking money from a baby.

That made Cleo really sore.

Sweet kids, nice parents - you lucked out.

Hope it's as good for you this Saturday.

← she didn't look like she hoped any such thing!

I know it'll be as good. What could go wrong?
The kids will probably go to sleep around 8:00, so
the last 4 hours Carly and I will be paid for watching
TV. That's a good deal! And before that all we
have to do is play games and read books. I've
heard that some parents try to take advantage of
babysitters and ask them to do stuff that has
nothing to do with their kids – like ironing or
oven cleaning – but the Reeses aren't like that.
Cleo must be getting them confused with another
family. Maybe the Fitches. Leah babysat for
them once and they asked her to rake leaves
and mow the lawn too.

she stood up to them - that took guts!
↓

You can have me watch your kids...

...or do your yardwork. Not both!

And DEFINITELY not both at the same time!

Leah told me she's fine with washing dishes or cooking for kids, but there are some lines she absolutely won't cross. Cleo said she won't even wash dishes — that's what the dishwasher is for. The most she's willing to do is put the dirty plates in the machine!

Extra Chores Tolerance Scale

Everyone is different! See where you fit on the scale!

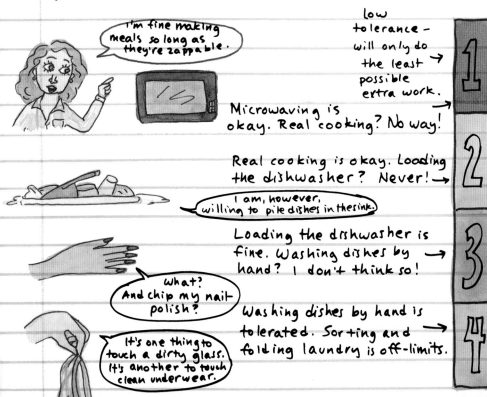

I'm fine making meals so long as they're zappable.

low tolerance — will only do the least possible extra work. → **1**

Microwaving is okay. Real cooking? No way!

Real cooking is okay. Loading the dishwasher? Never! → **2**

I am, however, willing to pile dishes in the sink.

Loading the dishwasher is fine. Washing dishes by hand? I don't think so! → **3**

What? And chip my nail polish?

Washing dishes by hand is tolerated. Sorting and folding laundry is off-limits. → **4**

It's one thing to touch a dirty glass. It's another to touch clean underwear.

If you're a 1-2 on the scale, you'll do the bare minimum. If you're a 3-4, you're willing to do a little extra. If you're a 5-6, can you come clean my room? If you're a 7-8, you can come clean my house!

I asked Carly to rate where she is on the Extra Chores
Tolerance Scale to check if we're compatible. I'm willing
to go as high as 6 — see, I don't mind hard work, just
difficult people. I admit I have no idea how to iron, but
I don't mind trying. Carly can iron, but she said she still
wouldn't do it. I'm more tolerant of chores. She's more
tolerant of brats.

I don't
mind hard
work, but I
have my pride.

If you
hire me to baby-
sit, that's what I'm
doing, not house-
keeping!

And since we're working
together, you're not doing that
stuff either! We need a
standard to stick to.

"Okay," I agreed. "So what's our standard?"
"We'll do work that has to do with taking care
of the kid, like making dinner and cleaning up
afterward, but no extra work. Not even something
easy like dusting or taking out the trash. Those
things aren't connected to babysitting."
I love that Carly's so clear about all this. She's
right — we'll be great partners despite our differences.

It's a good thing we set our standards, because now we have 2 jobs lined up. Mrs. Silvano, a friend of Mrs. Reese, called today and asked if we could watch her baby tomorrow night. Her regular sitter canceled and Mrs. Reese recommended Carly and me. Cleo is FURIOUS.

I give you a couple of jobs and now you're stealing work from me.

What am I? chopped liver? Don't I count?

Why didn't Mrs. Reese give Mrs. Silvano my name? I'm way more experienced than you!

I tried to calm her down.

"Probably because Mrs. Reese knows you won't change diapers — which isn't like washing dishes, you know. It's part of taking care of a kid."

"Suddenly YOU'RE the expert, telling me what I should do!" Cleo roared. "I'm GREAT with babies, even if I don't change diapers. I mean - GROSS!! They don't pay me enough for that. That deserves HIGH hazard pay. And who says a baby can't sit in its own juices for an hour or so? A little marinating never hurt anyone."

Hold you? NO WAY!

P.U.! I could just imagine being around a stinky baby that long. You'd have to handle the kid with special tongs to keep the stench far away. →

Goo!

Luckily for me, Carly says she'll handle any stink-bomb diapers. All I have to do is provide the expertise, since I have more experience with babies because of taking care of my half brother, George. That's more than Carly's done. She hasn't actually changed a diaper yet, so she has no idea what she's getting herself into. I sure do! And I know that babies aren't all the same—I've met George's baby buddies from day care.

TYPES OF BABIES

There are many sub-categories, but these are the 4 basic types. Avoid the Screamer and you'll be fine.

The Screamer— easily recognizable by her bright red face. Nothing makes her happy. Everything enrages her. You're left feeling totally helpless.

← The Smiler - it's amazing how a happy baby puts everyone around in a good mood. Even changing diapers isn't too bad with this cutie.

The Sleeper - if you're → lazy, this is the baby for you. You don't have to do anything, just be there in case of emergency— like an urgent need to raid the fridge.

I won't even go into the pacifier-addict type, since that's a subset of the Screamer. It's enough to say that with this kind of baby, a lost pacifier is the basis for WWIII—full throttle screaming.

Will that Screamer ever shut up?

this is George's type →

The Energetic Mover — this baby ← can be a charmer but a lot of work. You'd be amazed how fast a baby can crawl! Good luck trying to change a diaper! you have to catch him first and then you need 6 hands for the job.

TYPES OF TODDLERS

Babies grow into these 4 basic types — again, the Screamer is definitely the worst.

← The Screamer — screamer babies often grow up into screamer toddlers, which are even __worse__. They can have tantrums for no reason at all and once they begin, there's NO stopping them. You need real patience to babysit this kid or a good set of earplugs or be really, REALLY desperate for money.

The Smiler — these are sweet, irresistible toddlers. They're fun to be around even if they like to watch food fall on the floor or ask you to play catch over and over again. They're the kind of kid who asks what I call the endless question. (No matter what you answer, they'll ask __another__ question until you finally say, like parents do, "BECAUSE!")

Bye, bye peas! Here come the noodles!

Why is the sky blue? Why do we have 10 toes?

Why is a ball round?

WARNING — Don't pick up whatever they throw and give it back because they'll just throw it again...and again... and AGAIN! Amusing for them, but not for you!

The Sleeper — toddlers don't sleep as much as babies, but if you're lucky, you'll have one who falls asleep right after dinner, leaving you free to watch TV.

The only bad part is putting pajamas on a limp body — no easy task, but better than a thrashing, high-energy kid.

George is growing into this. Babysitting him will <u>really</u> be work!

Look at me!

Don't move an inch!

The Energetic Mover —

even worse than the energetic baby because now she can walk and climb and pull stuff down and get into some real tricky spots. WATCH OUT! If you look away for a minute, the kid can be out the door and in the street before you know it!

Let's play statue. You're it — now be still as a statue!

I showed Carly the baby and toddler types and she was impressed.

"Let's hope the Silvano baby is a sleeper," she said.

"If she's a screamer, we could call Cleo and let her take over," I suggested.

"No way!" Carly said. "I'm not going to be beaten by a baby!" I didn't say anything, but I know how horrible a difficult baby can be. She may be smaller than you and not know how to talk, but the power of her screaming can make the strongest grown-up feel completely powerless.

Please stop crying! I'll do anything! PLEASE!

WAAAH!

And a toddler having a temper tantrum? Forget it! There's no calming that storm. You practically need riot gear once he starts throwing cups, toys, food, anything he can reach.

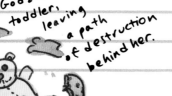
Godzilla toddler, leaving a path of destruction behind her.

So I was a little worried about the Silvano baby. Carly and I got to the house early — me because I was nervous, Carly because she was eager. It turned out to be a good thing, since Mrs. Silvano had a lot of instructions. I felt like I should be taking notes.

She's a very easy baby, but if she fusses, walk around with her. And sing to her — that usually works. Or you can try rocking her for a while or

Make sure her bottle is warm, but not hot, and there's some rice cereal if she's still hungry. If the house gets too cold, the thermostat is in the front hall, but don't set it above 7

It all seemed like basic stuff we already knew anyway (or was easy to figure out), so I don't get why she bothered to give us so many details. She acted like she was handing over a delicate electronic device with a 500-page instruction manual instead of a simple baby. I mean, all a baby does is cry, eat, poop, and sleep. How complicated is that?

Then she kept on saying she was going to leave, but there was always one last thing she had to say. Finally, after doing that 6 times, she really did leave.

After all that, the baby slept the whole time her mom was gone. Maybe she was exhausted by all the instructions. I know Carly and I were pretty tired of the walking, talking user's guide.

We ended up playing cards. It was a totally easy job. I mean, the babysitting part was easy. Dealing with Mrs. Silvano was another story. And I didn't get a chance to show Carly how good I am with babies. I wanted to impress her. I hope I get another chance.

We're so lucky! she's still asleep.

Yeah. We don't even have to change a diaper.

Maybe Carly was right — I worried too much over nothing.

I didn't get to show off my baby expertise, so I made some new guide pages instead. I knew Carly would love them.

TYPES OF PARENTS

Just like babies and kids fit into several categories, so do parents.

Our little darling never makes messes.

She cleans up after herself all the time! You'll see.

She's a real angel!

Doters - these parents think their kid can do no wrong, which is fine if their kid is a Smiler or a Sleeper. Otherwise, watch out! You'll get blamed for everything!

If my parents come home and find this mess, you're in trouble! They know their little sweetiekins NEVER makes a mess, so it's all y_o_ur fault.

Maybe it's time your parents learned what an "angel" you really are! I'm no_t picking up after you.

Believe me, this tactic won't work. No matter how much proof you have, the parents will be → mad at y_o_u, not their kid. You can't change that!

Rule-bound — these parents are like certain teachers. They have looooong lists of rules and there's no way you can keep them all. These parents are never satisfied, no matter how clean you leave the house or how long their kid's been asleep by the time they come home. Nothing you do is enough.

We keep the rules posted on the refrigerator. Make sure you read them all. Play time lasts exactly 20 minutes. Then it's time for something educational — it could be reading, math games, or listening to Mozart. Remember, no snacks before dinner and, of course, no dessert until every vegetable is eaten. Make sure teeth are thoroughly...

If it's exhausting for you, think of → what it's like for the poor kid!

Generous — these parents are the best. They aren't too demanding and they know how to make a babysitter feel welcome. In fact, they know how to make babysitting feel like a mini-vacation.

Help yourself to whatever you want in the kitchen. We ordered a pizza for dinner and there are plenty of snacks. Once Callie is asleep, you're welcome to use our hot tub — it's very relaxing.

Nervous — these parents are kind of like the rule-bound ones, but with an added anxious edge. They're the ones who constantly call to check up on how their kid is doing. Or they have problems leaving, like Mrs. Silvano. They can't quite trust you to babysit.

He's fine — just like he was 5 minutes ago.

And 5 minutes before that.

No, he isn't running with scissors. He didn't drown in the bathtub. He didn't choke on his dinner. HE'S FINE!!!

Taskmasters — these parents think babysitting is a cushy, easy job and they're not getting their money's worth unless you do other work for them. Either be clear about what you're willing to do or be prepared to work your tail off.

Here's the mop for scrubbing the floor. Don't forget the laundry and clean the oven too.

Am I a babysitter or a slave?

I'm getting better with little kids and their parents, at least in this guide (where I'm storing up experience). But I still have the most experience with babies, so I made this quiz for Carly to see where she fits on the range of babysitters from Cleo to me. (Although I already know she's NOT like Cleo!)

QUIZ #3

WHAT KIND OF BABYSITTER ARE YOU?
(for babies, not older kids)

① What do you like to do with little babies?

ⓐ Play peek-a-boo and talk baby talk.	ⓑ Cuddle them.	ⓒ Watch them sleep.	ⓓ Nothing.

ⓐ Where am I? Can '00 see me? Can '00?

ⓑ Ah, the smell of fresh baby! It's like the smell of fresh-baked bread (as long as their diaper's dry).

ⓒ That's an angel, just what I like to see. Now I can call my friend.

ⓓ Here you go, in baby jail!

④ What's the perfect temperature for a baby's bottle?

ⓐ Exactly 81.5°.	ⓑ Not too hot, not too cold, just right.	ⓒ Refreshingly cold — adding ice cubes helps.	ⓓ Whatever it is — babies aren't picky.

⑤ What's the perfect food for a baby?

ⓐ Whatever you can clean up easily.	ⓑ Whatever you can mush or strain.	ⓒ Whatever you can get them to eat.	ⓓ Pizza!

6. When is it a good time to put a baby to bed?

(a) When you need to clean up the mess from dinner.	(b) When the baby is tired.	(c) When you're tired.	(d) When your favorite show comes on.

7. What's the best way to get a baby to fall asleep?

(a) Bore him to sleep by reading homework out loud.	(b) Rock her to sleep while singing a lullaby.	(c) Tuck him in his crib.	(d) Lull her to sleep by watching your favorite show.

(12) What do you tell the parents when they come home?

(13) What do you tell the parents when they ask you to babysit again?

If you answered mostly a's, you're careful and fastidious, neat and clean. You're fine with babies, but you're even better organizing closets — just like Leah.

Leah's a talented artist, a loyal friend, and a neat freak.

If you answered mostly b's, you're warm and friendly and get along well with babies. If you had a friend with you, then everything would be perfect. You're like me!

Carly said b's, like me — does that mean she doesn't need me?

If you answered mostly c's, you're practical but more interested in your own comfort than the baby's. Another job might fit you better. You're like Gigi.

Gigi is Cleo's best friend. She's very stylish and elegant — which is good in itself, but not good for babysitting. She's too worried about chipping her nails to take great care of a baby.

If you answered mostly d's, you're too selfish to be a good babysitter. You need to think about the kid every now and then, not just stuffing your face. You're like my sister, Cleo.

Hey, my only problem is I don't do diapers. Big deal!

When Cleo heard that we didn't even have to change a diaper at the Silvanos, she was madder than ever.

It's not fair! You've had 2 easy jobs in a row. Babysitting isn't like that, you know. There are brats out there. And crazy parents.

I told her Mrs. Silvano wasn't exactly easy, but I had to admit she wasn't horrible, either. She just talked too much. That kind of thing is easy to ignore, especially when there's money at the end of the day.

I didn't want to do this, but it's time you heard some babysitting horror stories. You need to know it's not all snacking and watching TV.

She didn't sound at all like she didn't want to do it. She looked thrilled to tell us a whole collection of Babysitting-Gone-Bad stories, things that happened to other kids, not just her.

I'm putting the best two in this guide.

Story #1:

Embarrassing Moments

(Naturally this is Cleo's story, told in her own words.)

Ahem, let me begin.

"I've never had a problem with kids. Despite what Amelia says, little kids LOVE me! And parents do too — really! I'm an expert, a pro, a natural babysitter."

"But everyone makes mistakes, right? We're all human, aren't we? Anyway, there was this one time I was babysitting Deke, a kid I'd babysat many times before. Since he was such an easy kid and I knew he went to bed early, I thought it would be okay to have my boyfriend come over. I mean, it's boring by yourself. And Deke's parents never said I couldn't have a friend over. Okay, I didn't ask, I admit that, but like I said, they'd never given me a rule against having friends visit. So Corey came over."

This is Corey (artist's rendition).

Corey? Who's Corey? Corey?!

Cleo's had more boyfriends than I can keep track of. How? Why?

What do boys see in her? I don't get it.

"And ya know,
we were getting comfortable because Deke was
sound asleep. That kid is sweet, never a problem.
So it was cool with Corey and me EXCEPT Deke's
parents came home earlier than they said they
would. It was pretty embarrassing — for them
more than for me."

"Well, actually for Corey — he sure turned red!"

Cleo wasn't sure
who was more
upset — Deke's parents
or Corey.

Cleo was fine, of
course. Nothing embarrasses
her.

"The end of the story is that Corey's not my
boyfriend anymore (no loss there) and I haven't
babysat for Deke since then."

So there's Cleo's story in her own words (with my
pictures). Somehow I don't think I'll ever have the
same problem. And anyway, the baby wasn't
horrible — Cleo was!

Story #2 : Difficult Moments

(This one is Gigi's.)

Gigi is Cleo's best friend, which you would think means she has terrible taste, but really she doesn't (except in her choice of best friend). She used to babysit a lot, but now she doesn't, all because of her WORST night ever.

> What's really surprising about this story is that normally I don't have ANY trouble babysitting — kids listen to me. So do their parents. I'm not the kind of person you mess with. Most little kids sense that. Not this one.

I'll let Gigi tell the story:

"I'm good at handling kids. They respect me and I respect them. Even bratty kids behave around me — or else! I have the magic touch. Or so I thought until I babysat for the Shrieking Terror."

"I would _never_ have said yes if I'd known how difficult this kid was, but as long as her parents were there, she was a perfect little angel."

"The second they drove away, she started to shriek. Just like that!"

WARNING: CONTINUED EXPOSURE TO THIS KID MAY BE HAZARDOUS TO YOUR HEALTH AND SANITY. TAKE ALL PRECAUTIONS!!!

She looks innocent, but looks mean nothing!

I didn't know mouths could open <u>that</u> wide! →

She was like a fire alarm going off — shrill, loud, grating, UNBEARABLE! ←

"One minute she's smiling and waving, the next she's yelling her head off."

"I tried EVERYTHING to shut her up! I offered to play a game, read a book, go to the park, draw pictures, bake cookies — nothing got through to her. She kept on screaming. I thought she'd shriek herself hoarse after an hour, but nope, she could go on forever. But <u>I</u> couldn't. I'd had it! So I called her parents and said I couldn't stay. They could hear the screaming in the background and they begged me not to give up. They said if they came home early, they'd be rewarding her bad behavior. I said maybe, but if they didn't, they'd be punishing <u>me</u>."

"So they offered to pay me TRIPLE my regular rate if I would hold out for just one more hour. I should have said no — NOTHING was worth another hour with the Screaming Meanie — but I said yes. I'm tough. I figured I could take it."

But I couldn't...
↘

Either my head would explode or the kid would. It had better be the kid! ←

"I picked up the Shrieking Terror, carried her, kicking and screaming, to her room, and shut the door. Then I turned the TV on really loud. It wasn't so bad that way. I watched a cop show with a lot of explosions and her yells blended right in."

"When the parents came home, she was still shrieking (but not as loud — she did get tired after all). I took the money and told them never to call me again. They haven't."

SHRIEKING TERROR
NOT WANTED:

DO NOT BABYSIT THIS KID! LOOKS SWEET AND NICE — IS NOT!!

"Now their kid is on my banned list. None of my friends will ever babysit her either."

I have to admit, I admire how Gigi handled this. I would have thought it was all my fault, that something was really wrong with the kid, that she was hurt or scared or something. And I had to fix it.

Luckily this is a very rare thing to happen. Kids can be a little bratty, but usually not this bad! I know Cleo wanted to scare me with this story, but we've been lucky so far playing Babysitting Roulette. And we'll never have Cleo's problem either!

"Nice try, Cleo," I said, "but the third time's the charm. I bet our 3rd babysitting job will be the best of all!" Actually, I didn't see how it could get any easier, but we would be making more money, lots more money.

I told Carly about Cleo's warnings and horror stories, but she just laughed.

"We know these kids, remember?" she said. "This isn't a game of Babysitting Roulette."

"Right," I agreed. "And we know the parents. They aren't a problem either."

"Plus we know what good snacks they have," Carly said.

"And cable TV," I added. "It's going to be a great Saturday!"

That's tomorrow. I can't wait until tomorrow night when I'll be rich, rich, RICH!

I would say I slept like a baby, except I had strange dreams of babysitting baby Cleo - yucch!

In my dream, Cleo looked exactly the same only she was a baby and she would NOT stop crying. Carly and I started screaming at each other because neither of us wanted to deal with her. We were all screaming.

We weren't being good partners. We were terrible. But it wasn't our fault — it was Cleo's. If she hadn't been such a brat, we would have been fine. That didn't stop us from yelling at each other, though. The dream ended when Carly finally grabbed Cleo, tucked her under her arm, and stomped off.

I was so relieved to wake up, I wanted to forget all about my bad dream. Carly and I are a good team and everything would be fine. At least, that's what I told myself.

That morning when we got to the Reeses' house, it was completely different from the last time we were there, just a few days ago. For a minute I thought I was still stuck in my nightmare — everyone was cranky and grumpy.

WAAAH!

NO! STOP! DON'T!

Tyler was crying because he spilled milk on his pajamas and he didn't want to change them.

Ruthy was mad because her mom was trying to brush her tangly hair.

Mr. Reese was yelling at everyone to behave and be quiet, they had to go. →

That's enough, kids! We're leaving. Amelia and Carly will help you out.

Mrs. Reese was embarrassed by it all.

Sorry, girls, to rush off like this. I'm sure things will calm down as soon as we leave.

Only they didn't. Calm down, that is. It was a bad start to a bad day and things just got worse.

It took 20 minutes to convince Tyler to change out of his milky pajamas, and as soon as he did, he spilled orange juice all over his shirt. That meant another 20 minutes of begging and pleading until he was in clean clothes. Carly wanted to be sure there would be no more messes.

This time if you're going to eat or drink anything, you're wearing a garbage bag first!

↑

She meant like a kind of giant bib, not that Tyler belonged in the trash.

But somehow what she said made an even bigger mess.

WAAAH! You're mean! you want to throw me away! you think I'm garbage!

I'll show you! I'm running away! You'll never catch me! Run, run, as fast as you can. You can't catch me! I'm speedy man!

While Carly was chasing after Tyler — he was surprisingly fast, just like he said — Ruthy was trying some fast moves of her own on me.

Since I brushed my hair like a big girl, I get my big-girl reward.

Mom always makes me a chocolate sundae and lets me watch a movie after I brush my hair. It's my big-girl hair prize.

Big goo-goo innocent eyes made me extra suspicious.

It seemed like making a really big deal out of a little wispy brushed hair, and I had the feeling Ruthy was lying. But I wasn't sure. So I made her the sundae and let her pick out a movie to watch. At least she wasn't running through the house and climbing the furniture the way Tyler was.

Carly finally tackled Tyler and told him for the 100th time she wasn't going to throw him into the garbage.

"Tell you what," she said, glaring at me. "Amelia will make you a nice chocolate sundae for breakfast like she made your sister and you can both watch a movie."

Was Carly annoyed at me because I didn't help her chase Tyler or because I made the sundae for Ruthy?

"I'm just trying to smooth things out around here," I said. "What's the big deal?"

"I don't think ice cream is the way to solve bad behavior." Carly's voice was colder than the mint chocolate chip.

"Okay, partner," I said. "Then you solve it." I headed toward the living room.

"Wait!" Carly called. "I'm sorry — we shouldn't fight. We have to work together." She started scooping ice cream into a bowl.

"Yay!" Tyler yelled. "Ice cream, ice cream, ice cream!"

"You certainly are screaming," I said.

Carly looked at me and laughed. Just like that we were friends and partners again.

We had to team up. We had to work together. Otherwise, things would melt down completely.

Tyler was happy with his sundae, but Ruthy wasn't. "That's not fair!" she wailed. "You only get ice cream if you brush your hair. Tyler didn't brush his hair!"

"You liar!" Tyler yelled. "You made that whole thing up to get a sundae."

"You're the liar!" Ruthy raged. She ran up to Tyler and kicked him.

"Stop it, both of you, NOW!" I grabbed Ruthy. Carly grabbed Tyler. It wasn't even 8 a.m. yet and I was exhausted. So was Carly. Unfortunately the kids had plenty of energy.

So we resorted to the time-honored, last-ditch resort of all babysitters (including parents). We parked them in front of the TV.

That gave us an hour of peace while we cleaned up the kitchen.

"I'm sorry I snapped at you like that," Carly said. "The most important thing is to work together, no matter what. Even if I don't like what you're doing."

"Even if," I agreed. "Especially if! We're going to handle things differently, okay?"

Carly nodded. Then the movie ended and our reprieve was over. It wasn't even 10 a.m. and Ruthy wanted lunch.

There she was with those big, begging eyes again. →

My tummy's hungry. Can I make a sandwich? Pleeeease! Mommy always lets me.

I didn't want her fooling me again, so I asked Tyler if it was true about the sandwiches. If I had to face another mess in the kitchen, there had to be a real reason.

oh, yes. <u>Whenever</u> we're hungry, we're allowed to make sandwiches. Any time of day. Mommy says that's better than snacking on cookies or chips.

He had big, innocent eyes too,

but what he said made sense. And since they'd had ice cream for breakfast, a sandwich sounded like a good thing, or at least a healthier one.

So I told Ruthy she could make a sandwich and naturally Tyler wanted to make one now too. It became a contest between them who could come up with the most original sandwich.

Ruthy's

← mayo
← sardines
← pickles
← left-over french fries
← baloney
← relish
← marshmallows
← cold toaster waffle
← cold hot dog
← salad dressing
← ketchup
← mayo

Tyler's

honey
pickles
cream cheese
salami
mustard
lime jello
chili beans

cold spaghetti
ketchup
tofu
peanut butter

It kept them busy, but the kitchen was a horrible mess again. The sandwiches themselves were a mess.

"Those are gross!" I said. "You're not really going to eat them, are you?"

"Of course not," said Tyler. "That would be rude. We made them for you and Carly."

Carly tried not to gag. "How sweet of you," she said. "I'm sorry I can't eat mine since I'm allergic to pickles, but I'm sure Amelia will love hers."

"Thanks a _lot_," I whispered to her.

Tyler and Ruthy looked at me with their big, big eyes.

I couldn't. Really. No matter how big their eyes were or how much I hurt their feelings.

 I decided to make my eyes as big as theirs.

You guys are SO sweet! These sandwiches are so, SO special, I want to save them and bring them home, so I can give one to my sister, Cleo.

That idea was a big success. They were so excited that Cleo would get one of their sandwiches, they even added an extra layer of grape jelly and peanut butter. Yum!

Unfortunately when it was really lunchtime, they refused to eat anything. Until we let them make toasted peanut butter and jelly sandwiches, which naturally meant getting sticky peanut butter and jelly all over the oven, table, chairs, floor, and walls. Carly even got some in her hair. I stepped in some. We may have been working as a team, but this day was really not going well. Every hour seemed to last 3 hours. I didn't see how we could survive until 8 p.m., when the kids would finally go to bed.

tick

tock

tock

tick

I thought watching the clock at school was agony.
I thought nothing could move slower

Every time we got the kitchen clean, it was gunked up again. I wondered if this would be our babysitting horror story.

than those hands. I was wrong. The kitchen clock at the Reeses was much slower. Time was practically standing still. Why do fun things feel like they happen so quickly and terrible things plod along at a snail's pace to make them even worse?

Between lunch and dinner we had 2 accidents, 4 messes, and one major disaster. Carly lost her temper twice and I lost mine so many times, I was sure I'd never find it again. This wasn't anywhere near the fun time we'd planned.

Mess #1: (I'm not even counting the kitchen messes.) Ruthy decided to play dress-up and took EVERYTHING out of her mom's closet (including

slip as bridal veil →

mom's makeup smeared all over her face. →

lace blouse as wedding gown →

some stuff I'm sure Mrs. Reese didn't want anyone seeing, like thong underwear).

clomping around in expensive high heels ←

Mess #2: Before we could stop her, Ruthy chewed up 2 lipsticks, muddied up 3 colors of eyeshadow, and dropped a mascara wand down the toilet.

Mess #3: Tyler was busy all this time in the garage. He spilled oil, paint, and sawdust all over, including on himself. He needed to change AGAIN and take a bath, which led to the major disaster.

Seeing the mess in the garage made Carly lose her temper for the first time. She'd been amazingly calm with Ruthy's stuff. With Tyler, she snapped.

What were you thinking?!

This stuff is DANGEROUS!! It's not for little kids, so don't tell me your parents let you do this! Tell the TRUTH!

Tyler looked sorry, very sorry.

"No, they don't," he admitted. "But I wanted to surprise them with a cool invention. Only it didn't work."

The only thing he invented was a gunky, smelly, hard-to-clean up mess.

I wasn't sure how to do it, but I started to clean up the garage while Carly turned on the water for a bath. It was a good thing there were two of us. I couldn't imagine dealing with these kids by myself. I wondered, how did Cleo do it? Was this why she'd warned us so much?

I couldn't wash away the oil stain, but I did the best I could. I felt like I'd been scrubbing things all day. Wait - that's because I <u>had</u>! When I slumped back into the house, Ruthy ran up to me, all excited.

"Look!" she yelled, pointing to the bathroom. Water was running down the hallway, flooding into the bedrooms. I sloshed through it to the bathroom. The bathtub was overflowing!

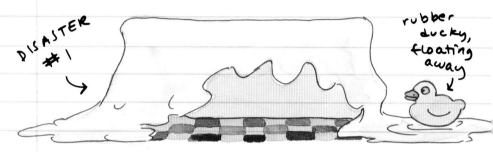

DISASTER #1 →

rubber ducky, floating away ↙

I turned off the tap and opened up the drain, but there was still water all over the floors. And where was Carly? I didn't have time to look for her — I grabbed every towel I could find to sop up all the water. I had to use all the towels in the house, even the washcloths and paper towels. By the time I was finished, my pants, socks, and shoes were soaked. And still no sign of Carly. Or Tyler.

"They must be outside," Ruthy said. "Tyler didn't want to take a bath, so he climbed the tree in the front yard. Carly went to get him down."

← towels, towels everywhere ↗

I couldn't face ANY more messes, so I took Ruthy with me and we both went outside to see what was going on.

Carly was just climbing down from the tree when we got there. Tyler was already on the ground. So were several snapped-off tree branches — mess #4 to clean up.

"You could have helped me!" Carly wailed. That was the second time she lost her temper. She was really mad, this time at me. "Look what happened!"

I looked. She'd scratched her face on a branch and tore her shirt. That was accident #1.

"I'm sorry," I said. "But look at <u>me</u>!"

My wet pants were dripping and my shoes made squishy sounds when ⟶ I walked.

"Oh no!" Carly groaned. "I forgot I left the water running!"

"Yes, you did." But I wasn't mad. I was relieved it was Carly's mistake, not mine.

"How bad is it?" she asked, not angry either anymore.

"Bad," I said. "A total disaster. But I've mopped up the water. Now we have a huge load of towels to wash."

I started a new bath for Tyler, keeping both kids with me, while Carly did the laundry, including my jeans and socks. I felt dumb sitting there in Mrs. Reese's way-too-big sweatpants, but I wasn't going to hang around in my underwear — that would have been disaster #2.

No way was I leaving the tub until Tyler got in and out of it, all clean. I made Ruthy stay with us and we played I Spy, which is hard to do in a bathroom, where there's not much stuff.

For all the messes and mistakes, I felt strangely calm. Maybe because the worst had happened, but it wasn't my fault, and Carly wasn't any better at handling the problems than I was.

Unfortunately for Tyler, there were no towels to dry him with, so I used one of Mr. Reese's sweatshirts. Not as good as a towel, but better than nothing.

Finally, finally, finally, everyone and everything was clean. All I had to do was wait for my clothes and shoes to dry.

Then it was time for dinner. I couldn't take another mess.

Neither could Carly. Luckily we found a frozen pizza, something easy to make. And Ruthy and Tyler said they'd actually eat it, another bonus. So nothing bad happened until after dinner, when I stepped on one of Tyler's robot toys he'd left on the floor.

Me, hopping up and down on one foot, in pain. →

That was accident #2. Now Carly and I both had Band-Aids. We really were well-matched partners, even in wounds. ←

not-so-innocent toy — all sharp edges →

← I'm lucky I didn't trip on the way-too-big sweat pants. Nothing like falling flat on your face to bring a day to a perfect end.

At 8 p.m. Ruthy and Tyler used their big, big eyes again and told us they were allowed to stay up until 9 p.m. But Carly and I were WAY beyond believing anything they said. We were <u>experienced</u> babysitters now (I mean, we'd experienced it <u>all</u>, as bad as it could get). We had those kids in bed at 8:05 and the lights out by 8:30.

After 13½ horrible hours, we could finally relax!

We sat on the sofa in a stupor.

"Is it really over?" Carly asked after a while. "Are we done now?"

"Oh, we're done, all right," I said. "The question is, will we ever do this again?"

"Was it really that bad?" Carly touched the scratch on her face. "Think of all the money we're making."

I thought of it. Was it worth it? I wasn't sure, but I did know one thing — if I babysit again, it won't be like <u>this</u>. I'll do things differently. I won't fall for stupid tricks kids try to play on me.

Then I started to laugh. I told Carly I was remembering all the tricks <u>I'd</u> played on <u>my</u> babysitters. I guess we're even now.

Babysitting Tricks

I KNEW AND LOVED AND PLAYED ON POOR, UNSUSPECTING BABYSITTERS!

Making up my own rules and saying they were Mom's.

I'm always allowed to sit this close.

mom says ice cream is a very nutritious meal.

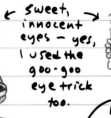

sweet, innocent eyes — yes, I used the goo-goo eye trick too.

I go to bed at 8:00, but I can read as long as I like.

Playing my own version of hide-n-seek.

Sneaking surprises under pillows — oh, that's where the peanut butter sandwich went!

Hiding books in the dishwasher — always check before turning on to avoid soggy pages!

Putting strange objects in the babysitter's shoe — plastic dinosaurs are especially painful and snails are especially gross!

Carly started laughing too. She had her own list of tricks she'd played. We both felt much better.

"You know," I said. "I was really worried that I'd let you down, not be a good partner, and you'd dump me — from the business and as a friend. Things were bad today, but that didn't happen."

"No, it didn't," Carly agreed. "We both made dumb mistakes, but we also helped each other." She grinned at me. "I couldn't have survived it without you, partner."

"Me neither, partner."

By the time the Reeses got home, I had my own dry clothes back on, and Carly and I had just finished watching a movie.

"How were the kids?" Mrs. Reese asked. "I hope they behaved."

Carly and I looked at each other.

"Oh, they did," I said.

"They went to bed right on time," Carly added.

"Great," said Mr. Reese. "Any chance you're free again next Saturday, same time, same place?"

We didn't even hesitate. We said it together, like the partners we are.

Of course!

And do we have a story to tell Cleo!